To _August & Carsten_

From _♡ Aunt Kathy_

Date _12- 25- 2010_

THE OLD-FASHIONED SANTA CLAUS
PICTURE BOOK

Copyright © 2005 Dalmatian Press, LLC
Based on *The Santa Claus Picture Book*, published in 1901
by McLoughlin Bros.

Published in 2005 by Dalmatian Press, LLC.
The DALMATIAN PRESS name is a trademark
of Dalmatian Press, LLC, Franklin, Tennessee 37067.
No part of this book may be reproduced or copied in any form
without the written permission of Dalmatian Press.

ISBN:1-40371-605-6 (B)
1-40371-759-1 (S)
14368

05 06 07 08 09 LBM 10 9 8 7 6 5 4 3 2 1

The Old-Fashioned SANTA CLAUS PICTURE BOOK

Compiled and Written by P.J. Shaw

The Magic of Santa Claus

Here's a nice little story for good girls and boys,
All about Santa Claus, Christmas and toys...

THE top of the Earth, which is called the North Pole,
Is where Santa Claus lives, a right jolly old soul!
About him the snow lies so thick on the ground
That the sun cannot melt it the
    whole summer round.

His twinkling eyes are so merry and bright,
That they sparkle like two little stars in the night.
He has rosy cheeks and the snowiest hair,
Though the top of his head is quite shiny and bare.

And each Christmas Eve, from his toes to his chin,
Santa's bundled up tight so the cold can't creep in.
His deer from the mountains are harnessed with care,
As they anxiously prance in the clear, frosty air.

Santa cracks his long whip
    and whistles a tune,
Then he winks at the stars
    and he nods to the moon.
And up, up away they soar,
    picking up speed,
For their magical journey
    each Christmas Eve.

On a starry night in December, Santa's trip begins.

The Reindeer's Flight

The reindeer take flight
with lightning-fast speed.
In fact, they're so fast,
you'd swear they had wings!
And these glorious reindeer
can easily fly
To the top of a roof,
no matter how high.

Then, down, down the chimney
Santa descends,
With a snap of his fingers,
a wink and a grin.
He has to be quick, to be through in a night.
His gifts must arrive before first-morning light!

So he fills up the stockings with trinkets and toys,
All without making the teeniest noise.
And with tinkling bells, on each snowy rooftop,
The proud reindeer wait—and keep the night watch.

Down, down the chimney, Santa descends.

A Wondrous Christmas Eve

Santa is cheerful but pleasantly shy.
(He likes to do all his good deeds on the sly.)
So there's no use in spoiling a long winter's nap
Attempting a peek at this jolly old chap.

No, when Christmas Eve comes you must slip into bed,
Pull up the covers and lay down your head.
Then Santa arrives with his magical pack—
A bag full of playthings slung over his back!

He gives to young children who live *everywhere*,
And the rich and the poor are alike in his care.
So great is his love for all girls chnd boys
That making them happy is what he enjoys.

Watching and waiting for Santa's sleigh.

The Spirit of Christmas

The most wondrous presents
    and toys are designed
For good little children,
    the gentle and kind.
And when Christmas comes round,
    as it does once a year,
It's certain that Santa will somehow appear!

How funny he looks as he sits on the floor,
Pulling out toys and then searching for more.
His cheeks are flushed pink and his eyes starry bright—
He certainly makes quite a comical sight.

His elves help him make such incredible things—
Monkeys and acrobats jumping on strings,
Footballs and baseballs and mystery games,
Chocolates and lockets and sweet candy canes.

And, oh! the dear dollies with long, curly hair,
That open their eyes or sit up in a chair;
With jackets and socks and the tiniest shoes,
And ribbons and hair clips that doll-babies use.

All the long year, with his paint and his glue,
Santa is making these presents for you!

Dollies with petticoats, buttons and bows.

Santa's List

Just in case you're longing to know,
These are the virtues good children must show:

Be hard-working at school
    and gentle at play,
Respectful to others,
    and kind through the day.

Not angry or sullen,
    snobbish or curt.
Not one to call names
    or say things to hurt.

Obedient, cheerful,
    and eager to please.
Not one to whine, or tell lies, or tease.

A child who has opened
    his heart to believe
That it's truly more blessed
    to give than receive.

Santa makes his list.

SANTA CLAUS'S PALACE AND TOY FACTORY·

The Crystal Toy Factory

To have enough playthings to fill up his sleigh,
Santa must work with his elves every day.
His workshop's a factory, so grand and so fair—
A real crystal palace set high in the air!
The walls are constructed of crystalline ice
That outshines the rays of the big Northern Lights.
And inside these bustling rooms all day long,
The elves do their work while they sing merry songs.

These good-hearted helpers know
    just how to make...
Trumpets and swords and the best roller skates.
Trains that can run on the tiniest tracks.
Soccer balls, marbles and fun jumping jacks.
Paint boxes, crayons and birds that take flight.
Puzzles and books to be seized with delight.
Soldiers and horses and pull-toys galore...

...Are hammered and sanded
    and sent out
    the door!

The workshop is such a wondrous place.

Toys and Treasures

NOW the workshop is such a miraculous place,
With stockpiles of satin and ribbon and lace,
Horses that gallop and dollies that walk,
And teddy-bears ready to cuddle and rock.

Games for all seasons, scooters and kites,
And books that talk back or pop up—what a sight!
Too many baseballs and footballs to count,
And two-wheeled, red bicycles ready to mount.

There are farmyards complete with their fences and trees.
Cows, sheep and oxen, all standing at ease.
Turkeys and ducks and fine chickens and hens,
And dear little piggies to put in their pens.

Each Noah's Ark is sent on its way
With nice little animals, ready to play.
Lions and tigers and camels and bears—
Two of each kind, since they travel in pairs!

Christmas Lullaby

IN a cradle so dainty,
a warm cozy nest,
Baby, sweet baby, is taking his rest.

Upon the white pillow his pretty head lies;
Closed for the night are his bonnie blue eyes.

The little hand's dimpled and pink as a rose.
And just what he's dreaming of, nobody knows.

Santa peeks at the baby, then leaves him a toy,
A cuddly soft doll for a small baby boy.

Then he tiptoes away, as the wee baby seems
To be floating away on an ocean of dreams.

Santa peeks at the wee baby.

Christmas Chorus

WE bless His birth
Who came to Earth,
and in His cradle lowly
Received the earliest Christmas gifts—
the Christ Child, pure and holy.

To Him we offer thanks and praise
for all the love He bore us.
For His dear sake, our hymns we make
in this, our Christmas chorus.

And while we deck these heavy boughs
with all our glittering treasures,
He from above will look with love
upon our simple pleasures.

He gave us friends,
our joy He sends,
He ever watches o'er us;
He bends His ear,
our song to hear,
And loves our
Christmas chorus.

Seeing and Believing

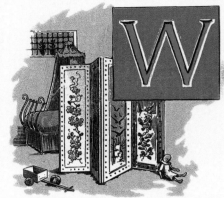

WHEN Jenny and Jessie woke in the night,
The moon and the stars cast
    a heavenly light.
And all of a sudden there came
    such a sound—
As if there were somebody moving around!

"It's Santa Claus—come down the chimney, I guess,"
In a wondering whisper, said Jenny to Jess.
"Oh, Jenny," said Jessie, "let's carefully sneak
Down the hall to the living-room doorway and peek!"

So they tiptoed like mice to the living-room door,
Making no sound on the hard wooden floor.
Then they drew back the curtain and looked in to see—
Sure enough! Santa! As plain as could be!

He stood near the fireplace, facing away,
And dozens of toys on the floor near him lay.
And since Jenny and Jessie made not one sound,
He kept at his work without looking around.

Did they speak to him? Dear, no! They trembled with fear
At the image of Santa Claus being so near.
One glimpse was enough, then they felt such a fright—
That back to their beds they flew for the night!

Christmas Festivities

GOOD Santa Claus sometimes,
    in making his rounds,
From a house brightly lighted will
    hear merry sounds.
And if he suspects that the laughter and noise
Proceeds from a group of young
    ladies and boys...

Curiosity, likely, will tempt him to creep
To some little window through which he can peek.
And there, for a while, he will longingly gaze
At the children who frolic in dances and plays.

And if some of the revelers happen to spy
Santa Claus watching so closely outside—
They'll tumble out laughing and squealing with joy,
And try to invite in the jolly old boy!

Santa Claus watches closely outside.

Sweet dreams on Christmas Eve.

Dear Santa,

Please bring me my own Christmas tree,
A sweet-smelling cedar,
    as big as can be!
With a dusting of snow
    and a tiny surprise—
A bird's nest that's tucked away
    on the inside!

Miniature pinecones and candles so bright
That they shimmer like ribbons of winter moonlight.
Crystalline snowflakes and silvery bells,
Tinkling just like the giggles of elves.

Bundles of cinnamon tied here and there,
And peppermint candy canes—plenty to share!
Garlands of marzipan, fashioned like fruit,
Sacks of rock candy, and sugar lumps, too.

Gingerbread sentinels all in a row,
Silvery tinsel and walnuts brushed gold,
Ruby red ornaments, shiny and bright,
And a star that will twinkle
with heavenly light.

—A star for the Christ Child,
   heaven's true light.

Christmas wishes sent special delivery.

Letters to Santa Claus

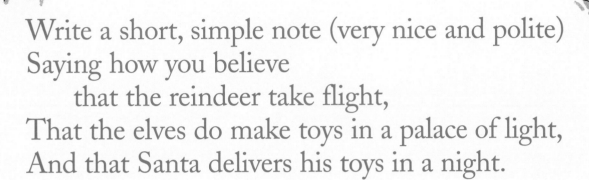

THE letters to Santa
    composed Christmas Eve,
Can be sent to him magically
    up the chimney!

Write a short, simple note (very nice and polite)
Saying how you believe
    that the reindeer take flight,
That the elves do make toys in a palace of light,
And that Santa delivers his toys in a night.

And list what you'd like to find under the tree
The very next morning. (Oh! what you'll see!)
    It's not like dear Santa to ever object
        To hearing of presents that children expect!

Out the chimney your letter
    will float on the air,
        And Santa Claus' helpers
        will capture it there.

Then they'll bustle
    right up to the
    Pole with great speed,
        Delivering letters to
        Santa to read.

Home at the North Pole.

A New Year Begins

When Christmas is over, old Santa Claus goes
To the frosty North Pole, for a well-earned repose.
He sleeps on a mattress of down every night,
As the polar star shines with celestial light.

And when he is rested and feeling quite well,
He goes to his shop for a talk with the elves—
About soldiers and dollies and soft, wooly lambs,
Telescopes, sailboats, and miniature prams...

And all year, he watches the children, no doubt,
To see if they tease, or say, "thank you," or pout.
He writes down their names on a page by themselves,
In a book that he keeps on his library shelves.

There's Emma, who tended the baby with care,
And Rachel, who braided her young sister's hair.
Steven, who likes to go smiling to school,
And Katie who tries to obey all the rules.

James, who behaves well—he minds what is said!
Joseph, his brother, who goes right to bed.
David and Isabel, now best of friends,
Who hug one another before the day ends.

Is Santa Claus happy? There's no need to ask,
For he finds such enjoyment, indeed, in this task,
That he bubbles with laughter and whistles and sings,
While imagining all of these wonderful things.

Giving is the secret of Christmas cheer.

Christmas Blessings

Who Santa Claus is,
    there's no need to tell.
Children around the world
    know him so well.

He comes like an angel
    of light from above,
To do on the Earth
    his sweet errands of love.

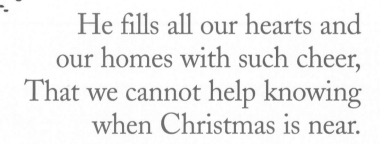

He fills all our hearts and
    our homes with such cheer,
That we cannot help knowing
    when Christmas is near.

Then let us be glad
    so that Christmas may be
A time of great blessings
    for you and for me.